TEN LITTLE ALIENS

MIKE BROWNLOW SIMON RICKERTY

ORCHARD

Ten little aliens need a place to stay.
Searching through the universe, home is far away.

Look – a sun with planets! Should they take a peep?
Ten little aliens all say,

"SQUEEP!"

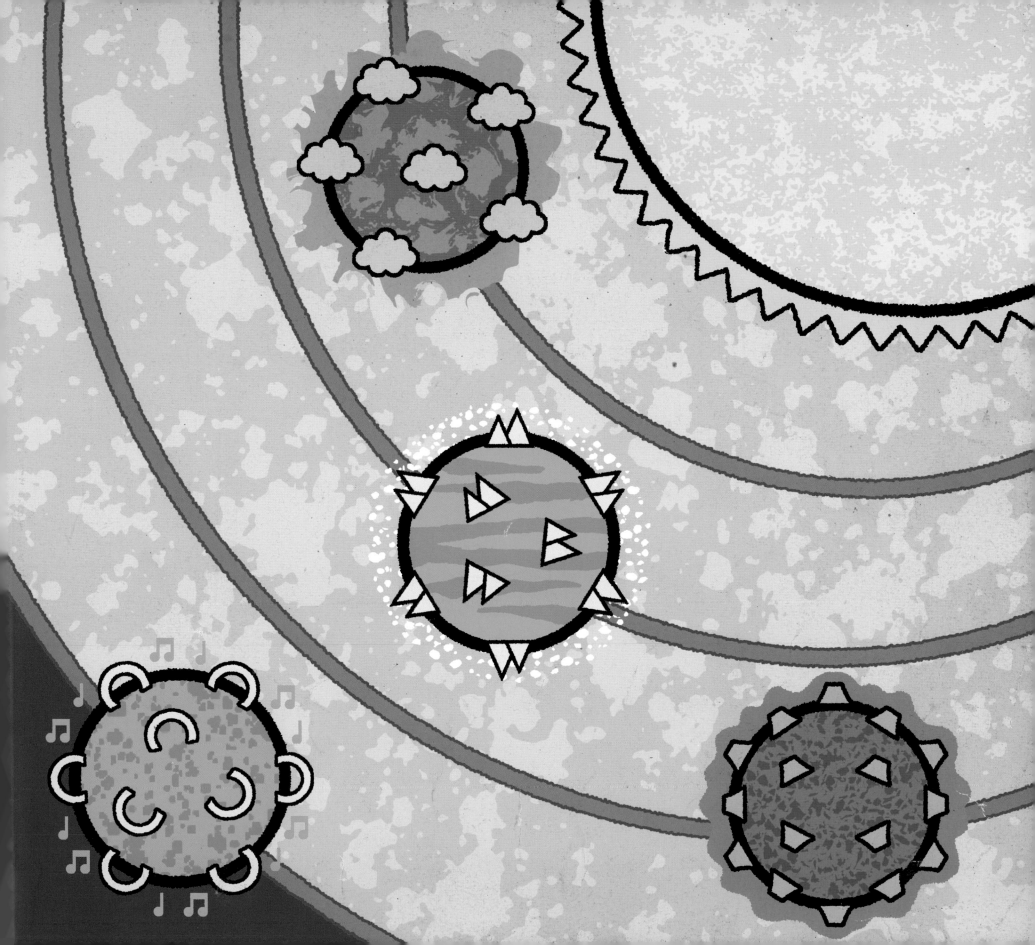

Ten little aliens, flying in a line.

FIZZ!

goes the comet's tail.

10

Now there are . . .

. . . nine.

Nine little aliens sniff
some plants, but wait –

9

SPLOOF!

go the Nova-Berries.
Now there are . . .

...eight.

Eight little aliens meet Mega-Robot Kevin.

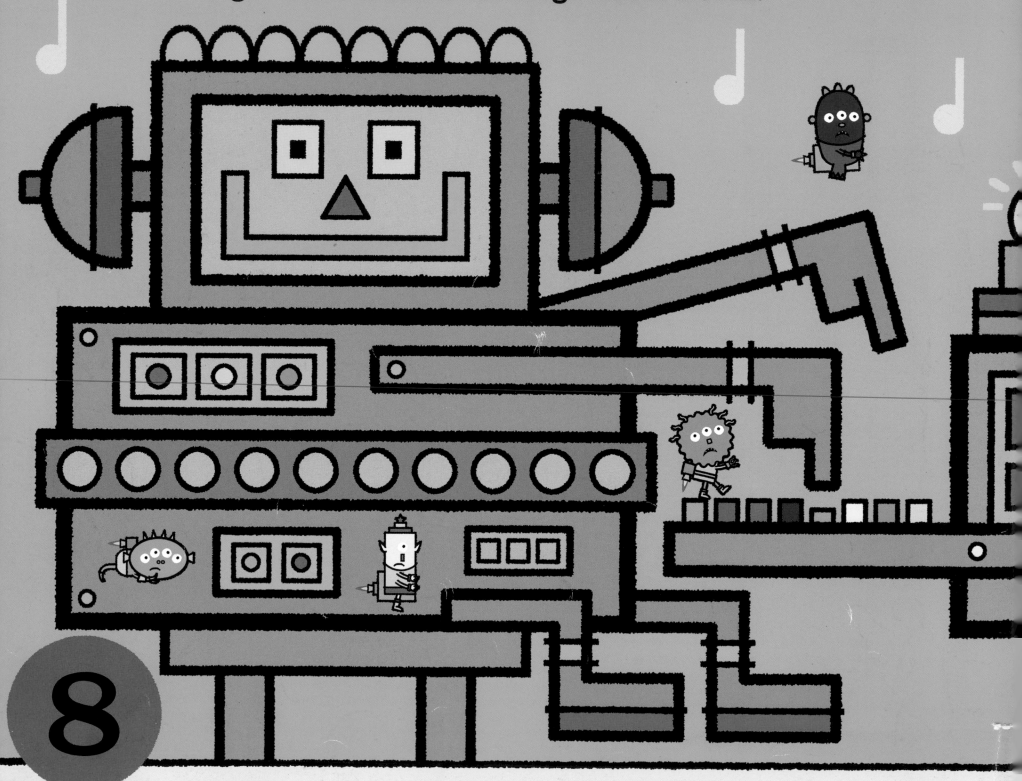

8

HONK!

goes his ampli-tron

Now there are . . .

. . . seven.

Seven little aliens in a fiery fix.

7

. . . six.

Six little aliens, shivering to survive.

"BRRR!

This p-p-planet's m-m-much t-t-too c-c-cold!"

Now there are . . .

. . . five.

Five little aliens hear a gruffly snore.

SNIFF!

5

"go the Snorkel Hounds.

Now there are . . .

. . . four.

Four little aliens have
to turn and flee.

4

BOING!

It's the Blobalobs! Now there are . . .

PARP!

goes the Trump-O-Tron.

Now there are . . .

. . . two.

Two little aliens, lost and on the run.

2

...one.

One little alien with
lots and lots to do.

ROAR!
goes the spaceship.
Time to save the crew!

1

One by one, she gathers up the
team that's left behind.

"It's too unfriendly here," she says.
"We've still got homes to find!"

So off they zoom for many miles,
searching through the stars.

Eventually they
fly past Saturn;
later whizz
past Mars.

But then they see a place they like —

a planet with a moon.

"Careful! Mind that astronaut!

Hooray! We'll be there soon!"

"It's such a pretty planet – all green and white and blue.

But are the people friendly?"

Well, that question's up to you . . .

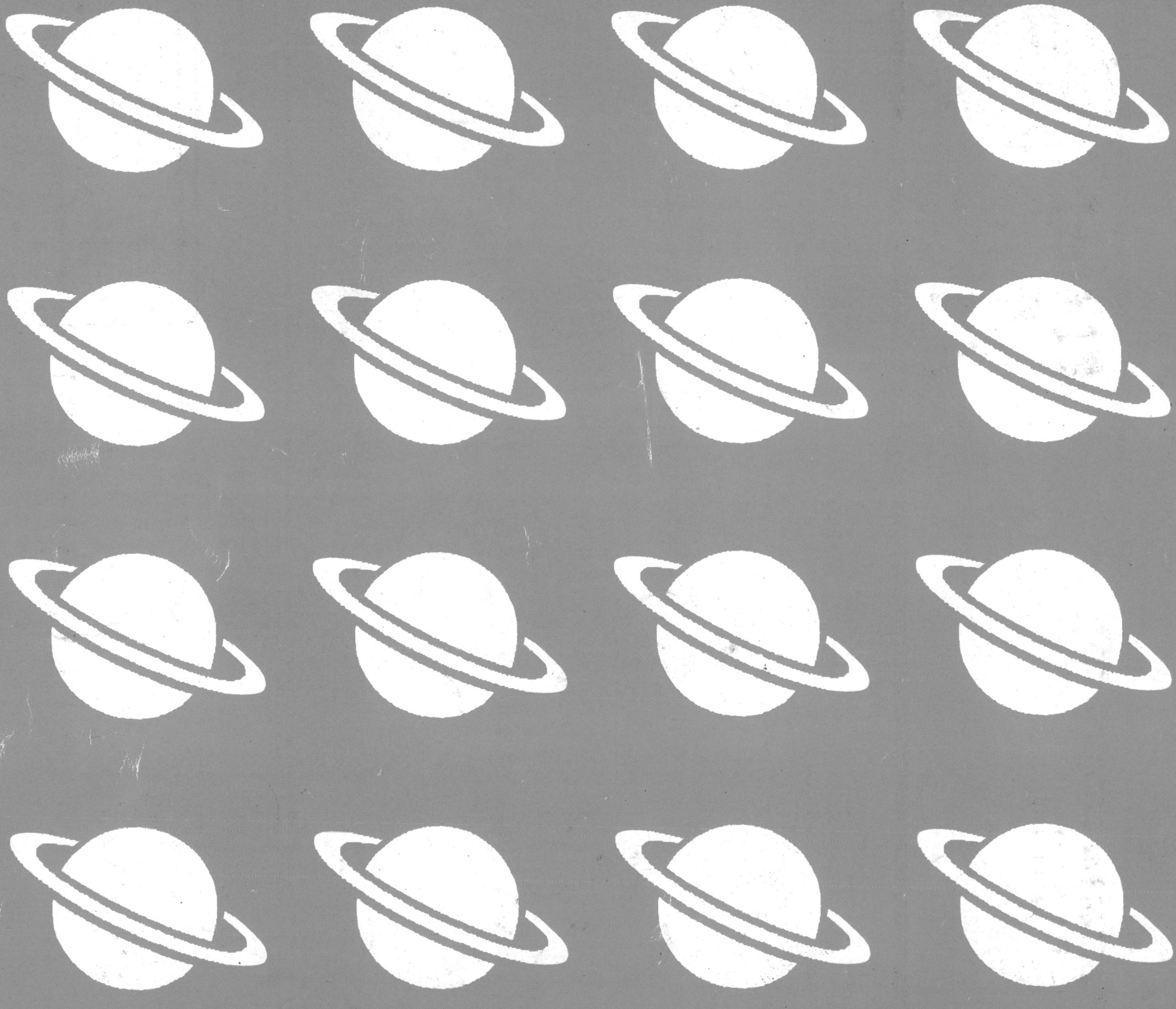